I loved the book it's 10 out of 10

Eira Roots, aged 8

I think the book is very good and here is a picture I drew

Lilith Roots, aged 10

There's quite a skill in writing a work such as this. Good choices of vocabulary and interesting use of adverbs; over all a fine effort!

Steven Rigby, aged 74
Former English Teacher
Northborough School, Maidstone

Wrapper the Rabbit
Adventures of Autumn

written by
Matthew G. Huggins
illustrated by
Bethany Rose Jones

Published by New Generation Publishing in 2021

First Edition

Paperback ISBN: 978-1-80031-020-9
Ebook ISBN: 978-1-80031-019-3

www.newgeneration-publishing.com

New Generation Publishing

www.mghwriting.co.uk

For Mum and Dad, thank you for the happiest
childhood anybody could wish for.

Wrapper was a wonderful and kind rabbit...at least according to five-year-old me, when one afternoon, I decided to staple nine pieces of paper together and have a go at writing my first book. Although spelling and grammar was questionable in one or two places, the fast-paced story with themes of friendship and adventure more than made up for it, and *Wrapper the Rabbit Makes Rabbit History* became an instant classic. Talks immediately began with my publisher (*Boo Boo*, my beloved stuffed rabbit; loyal friend and most trusted advisor) for a sequel. Sadly, despite our best intentions, we decided to play outside, and Wrapper seemed destined to remain a one-off.

Flash forward some twenty years, to a bright, blue skied afternoon walk through the grounds of the National Trust property, Scotney Castle. A particularly beautiful and inspirational little valley, with the river Bewl running through the middle, home to all manner of animals and even more plant life. As you cross a small stream and make your way up a short but fairly steep hill, eventually an oak tree with a particularly inviting swing beneath will appear before you. So, there I sat, and looked out across the green landscape. You know who might like it here? An old rabbit that I used to know. And so it was, that Wrapper made his long-awaited return....

I am pleased to say that I have found Wrapper to still be a wonderful and kind rabbit, although in the intervening years his taste for adventure seems to have grown somewhat. We can now follow this excitable young rabbit and his best friend Bea on their various ventures, as they explore the natural world around them, make many new friends and get themselves in (and thankfully out) of trouble, whilst the season of autumn falls across the picturesque valley all around them.

Younger me once described Wrapper the Rabbit as '*very exsitin*', and I hope that his return to page, imagination and heart, proves to be just as enjoyable. Indeed, after discussing this first instalment with my most trusted advisor (whom I am pleased to say is still around), he assures me that the themes of friendship and adventure remain at the stories heart. We were also pleased to find that Wrapper still has just as much of an appetite for dandelions as he ever did!

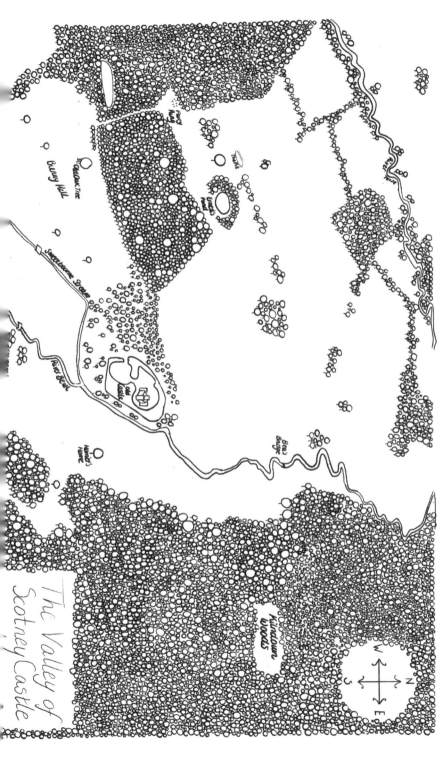

The Fall of Autumn

As autumn falls upon the hill
The world shall stop and stare
As leaves turn brown and tumble down
Leaving twisted branches bare

The air grows chill though winds are still
As the sun bleeds into the dawn
The ground a blaze with a colourful haze
A mist hanging over the morn

As acorns fall and mushrooms rise
The dormouse settles down
Feathers fly to warmer tides
The dark draws in around

The days once long seem all but gone
As autumn sings its song
But this is life; from day comes night
Let us all just dance along

Wrapper the Rabbit
&
The Adventures of Autumn

Adventures of Autumn

Matthew G.
Huggins Betheny
Jones

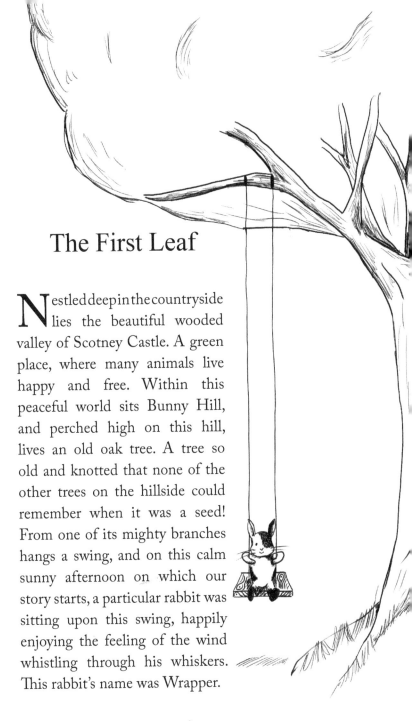

The First Leaf

Nestled deep in the countryside lies the beautiful wooded valley of Scotney Castle. A green place, where many animals live happy and free. Within this peaceful world sits Bunny Hill, and perched high on this hill, lives an old oak tree. A tree so old and knotted that none of the other trees on the hillside could remember when it was a seed! From one of its mighty branches hangs a swing, and on this calm sunny afternoon on which our story starts, a particular rabbit was sitting upon this swing, happily enjoying the feeling of the wind whistling through his whiskers. This rabbit's name was Wrapper.

Wrapper was not a particularly big rabbit, as he was still rather young, with black and white fur and a cute fluffy tail. Nonetheless, Wrapper was very brave and loved to explore. As he looked up at the tree swinging back and forth above, he gazed at the leaves in wonder. It seemed to Wrapper that there were simply too many to count (but then again, he could only count to ten).

He looked closer and noticed that some of the leaves had started to change colour. Then, before Wrapper's own eyes, a single brown leaf fell and began fluttering toward the ground. If Wrapper wasn't concerned before, he certainly was now. He jumped off the swing and tried to catch the leaf, meaning to put it back on the tree. Just then, the breeze blew out a big breath, and the leaf swirled and twirled away down Bunny Hill.

Uh–huh, an adventure! Wrapper thought with excitement, *I must get the leaf back, for the Old Oak will surely miss it!*

4

The leaf danced down the hill and Wrapper hopped quickly behind. As he raced, he caught a fluffy brown shape out of the corner of his eye. Wrapper stopped, pointed his ears toward the fluff, which also had a cream-coloured tail, and twitched his nose. With delight, he realised that the brown fluffiness was his best friend in the whole wide world, Bea.

Wrapper called out to her. "Bea! Bea! Over here!" She looked up, saw Wrapper, and hopped over. They quickly touched noses, as rabbits do when greeting each other, and before Bea could say a word, Wrapper continued, "Quickly, there is a matter of great importance, and its heading down the hill!" Poor Bea didn't even get a chance to reply before he was off.

As he flew after the leaf, he looked over his shoulder and was delighted to see his best friend running behind.

"Wrapper," Bea called out, "what's happening? Why are we running?" She was not always as ready for adventures as Wrapper, although she usually ended up coming anyway. This was handy, because she was tremendously clever, exceptionally kind and had helped Wrapper out of many sticky situations.

"A leaf! A leaf has fallen!" Wrapper shouted back.

Bea looked shocked and suddenly understood the severity of the situation.

The leaf was just ahead. They saw it fly across the bridge over the Sweetbourne stream, which ran along the foot of Bunny Hill. Wrapper, eyes on the leaf, cleared the bridge with a single hop. *THUMP*, went Wrapper as he landed face first, into an unexpected pile of wooliness.

Behind him, Bea screeched to a halt. "Hello Mrs Woollencot," she said to the startled sheep, who had leapt up with surprise, "Sorry about Wrapper."

"Why in the world are you in such a hurry?" bleated Mrs Woollencot, her face peering from beneath her white, woolly fringe.

Wrapper picked himself up, "There's a leaf! Sorry Mrs, I didn't mean to land on you but there's a leaf!" With that, he bounced off again.

Bea looked back at Mrs Woollencot and said apologetically, "There's a leaf." The sheep watched them hop away, very confused.

The two rabbits hopped through the sheep field, as the leaf danced on the wind across the grass. It soon made it all the way to the other side, over the next bridge and out of sight. The rabbits stopped. This bridge crossed the river Bewl and was much bigger. They had never been across before, and had no idea what was on the other side. Wrapper thought for a moment. He knew what he must do. He plucked up his courage and boldly hopped across. Bea followed, hesitantly.

Wrapper and Bea found themselves in the dappled shade of tall trees; but where was the leaf? Wrapper searched urgently around, whilst Bea twitched her ears nervously. Then, he spotted something. There, sitting a-top a great brown rock, was the Old Oak's leaf! With great relief, Wrapper leapt up onto the rock.

"*MOOOOO*" yelled the rock, as it stood up beneath him. Wrapper, together with the leaf, toppled off.

Bea hopped over to make sure he was okay, "You really should watch where you bounce, Wrapper." The two of them stared up into a pair of large, shiny brown eyes.

"You woke me! Why did you wake me? Do you know how long I've been trying to sleep?" mooed the cow angrily, a thick fringe hanging from between two large curled horns. The rabbits hung their heads apologetically. "Well?" he demanded again. Bea looked anxiously at Wrapper.

He sat up as tall as he could, but braver than he felt, and managed to say, "There was a leaf," and twitched an ear toward the leaf in question.

"A leaf? A leaf? You woke me, for a leaf!" The cow snatched the leaf off the ground and swallowed it whole.

"No, my leaf!" yelled Wrapper, before he could help himself. The cow glared at Wrapper, who fell into a sulky silence.

He yawned, and looked down sadly at the flattened patch of grass in which he'd been resting.

"Sorry, Mr," said Bea quietly and added earnestly, "We didn't mean to wake you."

"I know," he sighed, "I'm sorry I shouted, but every time I nod off a strange noise wakes me up and I have to start all over again." His tired eyes looked up into the branches, "I just can't see what it is. Oh, where are my manners? I'm Clarence, how do y...arghh, there it goes again!" They paused to listen. All they could hear was the whistling of the wind, and the soft gurgle of the river behind them.

"Clarence," said Bea softly, "I can't here anyth-" *TAP-TAP-TAP-TAP*.

The noise came loudly from overhead. Everyone quickly turned their faces upward, but all they could see was the gently swaying branches.

"*Moooo*," Clarence grumbled irritably. "You see? I can't sleep with that racket going on. I wish that it would go away!"

Wrapper, who had been silently stewing, suddenly sat up tall. "Uh-huh! This must be why the Old Oak dropped its leaf! Clarence, I promise to find out what is making the noise," Wrapper said importantly.

The cow looked doubtfully at Wrapper. "Try if you like little rabbit, but should I finally sleep, please don't land on me again," he said, as he settled back down. *TAP-TAP-TAP-TAP*, came the noise again, but this time, from beyond the trees. With a hop and a skip Wrapper was off in pursuit, the wind in his ears once more.

Eventually, they came to a halt, in the middle of a grassy plain. Bea sniffed the air as Wrapper looked around. They searched and they searched but could find no sign of the mysterious tapping. However, they did find several holes in the ground. They were like rabbit holes, only much bigger. As the rabbits looked closer, they heard movement. Their ears twitched instinctively and, out of the darkness, two bright eyes appeared. They both jumped back in surprise. Out from the hole trotted a very strange looking animal. Larger than a rabbit with a long pointed snout and a striped face, with scruffy black and white hair covering its body.

"Well, there's the look of two young rabbits who have never seen a badger before," she giggled. "Hello, I'm Harriet, and you two are a long way from Bunny Hill. Might I ask what you are doing this side of the river?"

So, Wrapper and Bea explained everything; the leaf, Mrs Woollencot the sheep, Clarence the cow and the mysterious tapping.

Harriet smiled a lot and laughed when they spoke of Clarence. "I know Clarence well," she said when they had finished. "Usually a lovely cow, but he does need his sle-" *TAP-TAP-TAP-TAP*, interrupted the sound again. They all spun around and found themselves staring at a great wall of trees.

"The Kilndown Wood," gasped Bea. The rabbits of Bunny Hill could see the Kilndown from the Old Oak, but not beyond. As far as they knew, it was endless. Every rabbit knew that you should never go in alone.

"But we won't be alone," said Wrapper, as if he could read Bea's mind, "we have each other."

Bea stared at him, hoping he didn't mean what she thought he meant. "We can't, it's too scary!"

Wrapper puffed up his fluffy chest, "I'm not scared of anything." Although as he looked back at the woods, the shadows beneath seemed to grow awfully dark.

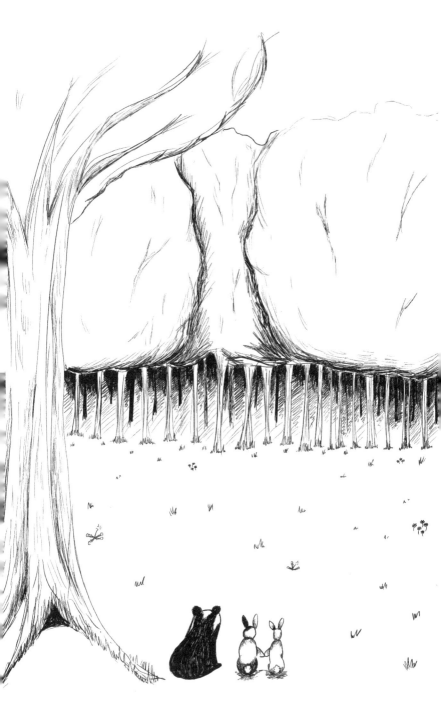

The trees were quiet. The rabbits hopped along silently behind Harriet, who knew the trails well. She had agreed to come with them, and they listened to the badger's stories as they went. She had roamed far and wide, beyond the boundaries of the valley. Even Harriet however, could not say where the Kilndown Woods ended.

"As long as we stick to the path," she kept re-assuring the rabbits as they followed the tapping sounds, which always seemed to be just a little ahead of them.

The trail started to slope upward and they began to climb. As the two rabbits hopped along, they looked around them. The bark was a deep mossy green and the floor seemed to be made of roots and fallen sticks. Plants they had never seen, smells they had never smelt and, most worryingly, far in the distance, very peculiar and unsettling noises they had never heard. Bea nuzzled into Wrapper nervously, who suddenly felt a long way from home.

The mysterious tapping continued up the hill. Eventually, they reached the top and the trees suddenly thinned. Wrapper, Bea and Harriet stood still and silent, waiting, listening. *TAP-TAP-TAP-TAP.* Off to the left, much closer than before. They ran over. *TAP-TAP-TAP-TAP.* Behind them, they ran back. *TAP-*

TAP-TAP-TAP. Just ahead now! *TAP-TAP-TAP-TAP.* To the left again! Now to the right! Now left again! Just ahead! Then, the tapping stopped. No sound. Nothing. Not even the wind.

TAP-TAP-TAP-TAP-TAP-TAP-TAP-TAP. Came the loudest tapping yet, so close they could almost feel it. Wrapper, Bea and even Harriet leapt with fright. They spun around. There, clinging to the trunk of the nearest tree…. was a bird.

They stared at each other. The bird was not like any Wrapper had seen before. It was bigger than most, its silky feathers were the same colour as the grass and its head was an even stranger colour, like a red berry! The bird blinked at them, looked back at the tree, and went, *TAP-TAP-TAP-TAP*, into the bark with its pointed beak.

"Sorry," it said quickly, and looked away.

Wrapper was confused, "What are you doing?"

"I can't help it," *TAP-TAP-TAP-TAP.* "I would stop if I could," *TAP-TAP-TAP-TAP.* "I know it annoys you." *TAP-TAP-TAP-TAP.* The bird looked away again, shamefully.

Understanding dawned across Harriet's face, "You're a Woodpecker."

"A what?" said Wrapper.

"What's a Woodpecker?" asked Bea.

TAP-TAP-TAP-TAP, went the woodpecker.

"I've never met one before! They peck at trees to make their homes and find food. Just like you burrow into the dirt and nibble at dandelions." Harriet turned to the bird and smiled. "Welcome to the valley of Scotney Castle, what's your name?"

TAP-TAP-TAP-TAP. "Walter", he said, lifting his head.

"What are you doing here, Walter?" asked Bea.

"Everywhere I go, people want me gone. They say I'm annoying, and that I should stop making such a racket or fly away. And I can't stop, I really can't! So, I fly aw-" *TAP-TAP-TAP-TAP*. "Sorry, my tapping gets worse when I'm nervous." *TAP-TAP-TAP-TAP*.

"It's okay Walter, don't worry," Bea said, smiling softly at him.

"Why were you running from us?" asked Wrapper.

TAP-TAP-TAP-TAP. "I was flying past, and I spotted the trees next to the bridge, with the cow resting beneath, and it looked so wonderful." *TAP-TAP-TAP-TAP*.

"I picked my favourite tree and started to peck, but I woke Clarence, and he looked very cross. Eventually he fell back to sleep, and I was going to wait, but I just got so nervous!" *TAP-TAP-TAP-TAP*. "I kept waking him up, and it just got worse, until-" *TAP-TAP-TAP-TAP*. "Then you arrived, and I heard him say," *TAP-TAP-TAP-TAP*. "He said he wished," *TAP-TAP-TAP-TAP*. "He wished that I," *TAP-TAP-TAP-TAP*. "That I would go away," *TAP-TAP-TAP-TAP*. Wrapper took in the terribly sad expression on Walter's face. "I just wanted a friend."

Wrapper paused for a moment, then said earnestly, "Walter, I'm so sorry. You can't help pecking, and there's nothing wrong with it either. We'll be your friends!"

Tap-Tap-Tap. "Really?" *Tap-tap-tap*.

"Yes," said Bea warmly. "Your tapping is part of who you are. You don't have to apologise for that."

"And we'll go have a chat with Clarence too," added Harriet with a smile. "He's a kindly old cow, and I'm sure he's finished his nap by now."

Walter the woodpecker smiled, eyes glinting. He gave a happy, *Tap-Tap*, on the tree.

Wrapper stood up tall and looked around. "Ummm," he said abruptly, "where are we?"

"The path!" exclaimed Harriet. "We've left the path!" Panic grew within the rabbits, and Bea began to thump her foot nervously. They suddenly noticed that the sky had begun to turn orange, and the tall trees were casting even taller shadows.

"We must be home before nightfall Wrapper, we must!" said Bea, with a look of terror flooding her face. The wind blew and Wrapper looked up. He suddenly saw what he had missed before. There were yet more strangely coloured leaves above his head. As the wind whistled through them, they began to fall toward the earth. Twisting and twirling, whirling and swirling, raining down around Wrapper until he was dizzy. He shut his eyes tight. He didn't know what else to do.

Bea's ear suddenly twitched, "Walter, how high can you fly?"

"All the way to the top of the trees," he replied, confused.

"Could you fly up, above the trees? So that you might see the way out? Then you can lead us with your taps, and we will follow you out, just as we followed you in!"

Walter swelled with pride, "Yes, yes, I can do that!" he flew off high and out of sight. Before long, they heard a *TAP-TAP-TAP-TAP*, just a short way ahead of them. The two rabbits looked at each other in relief. Oh, how glad Wrapper was that Bea was his best friend.

As they burst back through the trees, into the open air, they were bathed in a golden glow from the setting sun. Wrapper and Bea looked at each other as they hopped back across the grass. Bea had dirt on her face, and Wrapper's fur was full of twigs.

The sound of flowing water grew nearer and they caught sight of Clarence, happily munching on some grass. The cow looked up as they approached, and Wrapper hopped forward importantly. "Clarence", he proclaimed, "today a leaf fell, but it did not fall for you." The cow stared, obviously confused. "The leaf fell, because someone was being misunderstood, and needed to be heard." Wrapper turned around to face Walter. Clarence looked at the woodpecker.

"Hello Sir, I'm Walter," said the bird shyly, "I didn't mean to wake you earlier." *Tap-Tap-Tap-Tap.* The cow blinked at the woodpecker through his shiny brown eyes as he listened to their tale.

"Now Clarence," said Harriet finally, "for many years I have seen you living happily beneath these trees. But surely there's space for a friend?"

Clarence thought for a moment, then smiled at the woodpecker. "Which tree was it that you liked?" Walter, delighted, flapped over and stood proudly next to his new friend.

Wrapper and Bea finally crossed back over the river, where Mrs Woollencot was still grazing. They hurried back through the sheep field and across the stream, as fast as their little paws would take them. Halfway up Bunny Hill, Bea stopped to say goodbye.

"Thanks for getting us out of there, Bea," said Wrapper gratefully.

"It was Walter that got us out," she replied with a tilt of the head and a twitch of an ear.

"Yes, but it was your idea. We would still be stuck without you," said Wrapper in earnest. Bea smiled at him, touched noses, and hopped away home, her shadow hopping across the hill next to her.

Wrapper reached the top of the hill and he saw the Old Oak before him. Scattered below were even more leaves that certainly hadn't been there when he left. He was puzzled, but at that moment his mother appeared, hopping toward him. She was a black and white rabbit, just like Wrapper, although perhaps a little fluffier, and went by the name of Mrs Claire Muddypaw.

"Wrapper!" she called out from beneath her favourite floppy straw hat. "Have you been on that swing all day? You'll get stuck there you will. Look at the state of your face, did you fall off? You're just like your father!" As she brushed him down with her paw, she continued with a loving smile, "Home time now Wrapper. We'll have some dinner, wash our ears, get into our pyjamas and have some wonderful dreams." Wrapper suddenly realised how hungry he was, and all thoughts of falling leaves were blown from his mind.

Later that evening, after a meal of delicious dandelions, Wrapper's father, Mr Graham Muddypaw, was tucking him in to bed. Wrapper looked at him nervously. "Dad, I need to tell you something. I wasn't on the swing all day."

Mr Muddypaw looked puzzled. "What do you mean, my boy?" he asked. So, Wrapper told him. He told him everything, about the Kilndown Wood, about Walter, about Clarence and most importantly, about the leaf. Wrapper's dad listened quietly, and once his son had finished, he thought for a minute. "Thank you for telling me, Wrapper," said Mr Muddypaw. "No matter how hard it may be, it is always best to tell the truth."

Wrapper looked relieved, and confessed finally, "I was frightened today, Dad. I didn't like it."

His dad put his arms around him and gave Wrapper a big hug. "It's okay to be scared," he said, looking at Wrapper as he continued, "and you had your friends by your side. With the help of your friends, you can do anything." The two rabbits touched noses, and Mr Muddypaw left Wrapper to sleep.

However, Wrapper found this rather difficult. He tossed and turned in his bed. A little while later, a slow shuffling sound came down the tunnel. It was

Grandrabbit, who came hobbling into sight, with the aid of his trusty walking stick.

"What are you doing?" asked Wrapper.

Grandrabbit paused, leaning on his stick as he did so. "I don't remember," he admitted. Grandrabbit was a wise rabbit, though a little forgetful, and Wrapper loved him very much. "Do you remember why you are awake, squire?"

"I have a question."

"Yes, little one?"

"Why do leaves fall?"

Grandrabbit looked thoughtful. "Leaves fall because they must. This is the way of our world. Change is the only thing that will always be the same. We just have to appreciate it as it comes." They touched noses, and the greying rabbit shuffled off to wherever he was going. Wrapper, satisfied, finally went to sleep, dreaming of his next adventure.

Foxes and Forgetfulness

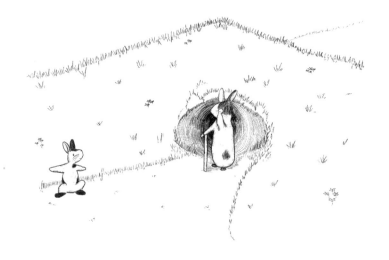

A cool dawn broke over Scotney Castle, the gentle sound of bird song echoing across the hillside as our feathery friends hopped amongst the crunchy leaves looking for any discarded nuts or berries. The rising sun dyed the sky a beautiful pink, casting a red glow over Bunny Hill, glinting off the morning dew.

Wrapper burst from the ground, sending an explosion of birds flying into the chilly air, shattering the peace. "It's time to go, it's time to go! It's morning, it's time to go!" He ran back down into the burrow, only to burst out again seconds later. "It's time to go, it's time to go. Come on it's time to go!"

Grandrabbit hobbled out behind him, walking stick in hand, bleary eyed and confused. "I really don't remember agreeing to this," he yawned.

Wrapper bounced around in excitement. "You did, I promise," said Wrapper, truthfully. Grandrabbit had promised to take Wrapper to his favourite little pond, but the old, grey and white rabbit was often forgetting things. Wrapper's mum said that it was on these occasions, that they must be extra kind.

Before they left Bunny Hill, there was somebody tremendously important they had to pick up. As they hopped through the morning grass, the sun slowly creeping higher, Wrapper's best friend in the whole world came into view. Bea was already waiting for them, below the Old Oak, rucksack on her back.

"I've packed us some dandelions," she explained as Wrapper looked at her bag.

They were on their way out of the village when Grandrabbit suddenly stopped. "Oh fluff," he whispered, as he ducked and sunk low into the grass. "Get down!" The two young rabbits copied, looking confused.

"Grandrabbit, what's wrong?" asked Wrapper.

"Ssshhh," hissed Grandrabbit. He twitched his

ears toward a patch of tall grass. Wrapper squinted.

Just ahead, he could make out some orange fur amongst the grass. As he looked closer, he saw a bushy tail and a little white pointed snout with a shiny black nose and whiskers.

"A fox," Grandrabbit muttered, "very dangerous." Suddenly the very dangerous fox jumped, as a butterfly

landed on the tip of its nose. The colourful insect fluttered around the cub's head, as it watched inquisitively, occasionally lifting a curious paw. Eventually the butterfly fluttered away, the fox bouncing after it.

As the three rabbits continued on their way, Wrapper spoke. "Grandrabbit, are you sure that fox was dangerous?" He tried to say this as nicely as possible, but the elderly rabbit frowned at the suggestion. "It's just he didn't seem particularly scary!" Wrapper added quickly.

Grandrabbit looked at both Bea and Wrapper sternly. "Foxes are the most dangerous things for us rabbits, they are nothing but bad news. They're mean, they're rude and most of all, they smell." The two friends looked at each other doubtfully.

The rabbits hopped joyfully through the woods in which they found themselves. Wrapper and Bea skipped and played together as they went, Grandrabbit smiling at the youngsters. As they reached the other side, the aged rabbit stopped for a rest and settled himself amongst the great twisted roots of a tall tree. Bea sat nearby and pulled a book on *Rabbit History* from her bag. Wrapper did not want to rest however, and decided to explore. He had been looking forward to this day for far too long.

Wrapper was having a good dig, at the foot of a large bramble bush, thoroughly enjoying himself, when he heard something move. He froze and twitched his ears. A soft crunching of leaves slowly plodded closer and closer, until it was right behind him. Wrapper turned, ever so slowly.

There, looking at him through big curious eyes, was the little fluffy fox. Wrapper jumped back in shock, cowering below the brambles. The fox leapt backward in response, tail dropping. Cautiously, Wrapper crept from his hiding place. He smelt the strange smell of the fox as he sniffed the air. The cub slowly stepped forward, one cautious paw at a time.

"Hi," said the fox uncertainly, in a squeaky, shaky voice.

"Hello," Wrapper replied, equally unsure. The two looked at each other.

A rustling sound came toward them and Bea hopped into sight, "Wrapper, Grandrabbit says it's time to go!" Wrapper looked back at the fox, but it had already vanished.

The three rabbits hopped along the grassy trail. Bea was looking for shapes in the clouds as she went, whilst Wrapper kept stopping to nibble at all the plants.

Upfront, Grandrabbit was telling them about the pond they were visiting. "Back in my day," he began, "rabbits used to visit all the time. We would hop up and down the edge, nap in the sun, play beneath the trees and splash in the water. Oh, it will be lovely to be back!" He paused to catch his breath, smiling fondly, leaning on his walking stick.

Bea stopped and stood next to him, "Why did you stop visiting?"

Grandrabbit looked thoughtful, as though he was searching deep into his memories. Eventually, a serious expression appeared upon his grey, fluffy face. "The foxes came." Wrapper looked at Grandrabbit curiously, who continued, "The day the foxes came, it was over. We couldn't play anymore. They made their dens near the water's edge and scared all of the other animals away."

"If it's dangerous… why are we going?" Bea asked, nerves creeping into her voice.

"Oh, the foxes are long gone now. They live deep in the Kilndown Wood, far away, but most rabbits are still frightened to visit."

Wrapper thought of the little fox. "But what about the one we saw earlier?"

"Just a lost cub. It's probably a long way away by now."

Wrapper said nothing. The fox had not seemed dangerous, although he wondered what might be waiting for them when they finally reached the water.

Wrapper was glancing around as they went, every so often looking over his shoulder. He saw no sign of the fox, but he couldn't shake the feeling that they were being watched. Suddenly, Wrapper jumped in shock as they turned a corner, making Grandrabbit drop his stick.

"What, what's the matter?" asked Bea quickly, twitching her ears in concern.

He felt silly. There was a large, cracked, mossy rock on the side of the road, but Wrapper had mistaken it for a full-grown fox waiting to pounce. "Nothing," he said in embarrassment, "That rock made me jump." Grandrabbit gave him a comforting pat on the back.

Bea however, was less sympathetic. "Wrapper, scared of a stone," she teased. "I'm going to tell everyone." With a little giggle, she hopped off, tail in the air, ears high.

"There it is!" Grandrabbit cried, raising his stick. Following its direction, the two young rabbits saw a blue, shimmering pool with luscious green grass and tasty looking foliage around the edge, dotted with a few trees. Bea gave a skip of excitement and bounded off toward the water. Wrapper, still thinking of the fox, followed at a much slower bounce.

"What's wrong squire?" asked Grandrabbit kindly. "You're unusually cautious, I'm surprised you're not paddling already."

Wrapper paused. "Nothing," he lied, and gave an unconvincing smile. Grandrabbit, satisfied, smiled back, and continued hobbling forward, happily whistling out of tune.

Bea reached the water's edge first and stuck in a tentative paw. She hopped back, fur standing on end. "It's very cold! I don't think we can paddle."

Grandrabbit gazed around fondly. He stretched and settled himself down. "Well, I'm going to have a little nap first, I think. You two stick together and don't go too far." As soon as the last word had left his mouth, his eyes closed and he started snoring softly.

The two rabbits hopped along, Bea testing the water every so often.

"Maybe it's never going to warm up," she sighed. She shot a sideways look at her friend. "Wrapper, what's the matter?" She knew something was wrong; normally he would have fallen in by now.

"Fine," Wrapper replied reluctantly, "but you must not tell Grandrabbit… the fox is following us."

Bea's ears immediately fell, "How do you know?"

"I saw it again at the edge of the woods, and I've felt like someone's been just behind us the whole way. Bea, what if the foxes are back?"

She looked terrified, "Wrapper, we must tell Grandrabbit! I'm sorry, but we must!" Before he could reply Bea had turned tail and hopped off, disappearing into the green foliage. This annoyed Wrapper. He knew Bea was right, but he hadn't wanted to spoil Grandrabbit's day out. Whenever he talked about the pond he would smile, and for a while, he seemed to become less forgetful.

Wrapper leant over and took a sip of water to calm himself. As he did, he caught sight of his cross looking black and white, fluffy face shimmering irritably back at him. Next to this familiar face was an orange and white, whiskered one, with two dark eyes and a shiny button nose, staring up at him.

The rabbit lifted his head up cautiously, and turned. Once again, he found himself face to face with the cub. This time Wrapper stayed calm, although his heart was pounding in his little chest.

"Hi," came the squeaky voice again.

"Hello," Wrapper replied once more. When the fox didn't continue Wrapper asked politely, "How are you?"

The fox gave a big smile, plonked its bottom on the floor, and scratched the side of its face with its back leg. As it did so, the cub toppled over ending up on its back, paws in the air, tail wagging. "Happy!" came the delighted little voice, still upside down. Wrapper's ear twitched, as two sets of paws came hurrying toward them. He sank low, guiltily.

Bea and Grandrabbit appeared. They both came to a shocked halt, eyes wide.

"Wrapper, get away from that thing!" said the old rabbit, with a look of fear.

Wrapper hopped closer, but stopped and looked back

at the fox, who was still rolling around happily on its back. "It really doesn't seem dangerous, Grandrabbit." The old rabbit wasn't interested however and leant forward to take Wrapper's paw. As he did, his stick slipped beneath him. He wobbled, he wibbled, and he toppled, with a cold, wet splash right into the water.

The rabbits jumped over in a panic.

"Cold, cold, cold," repeated the soggy rabbit, as he struggled to drag himself out, "cold, cold, cold." Wrapper and Bea grabbed a paw each and pulled him onto the dry grass. Grandrabbit began to shiver, and looked up at them, confused. "What happened?

Where are we? Why are we here? What's that?" looking at the fox, and as he looked at Bea, "Who are you?"

"We need to get him home, now!" exclaimed Bea. "Take my paw sir, it's okay." Grandrabbit looked at her anxiously but reached out to her with a shaking paw. Wrapper felt awful. He had ruined their special day. Not only was his Grandrabbit scared and cold, he now seemed to be more forgetful than ever.

"His stick!" shouted Wrapper suddenly, noticing that

it was missing, "I need to find his stick! You get going, I'll catch up." Bea nodded, face full of worry, as she led the sopping rabbit slowly away.

Wrapper searched everywhere. He looked through the grass, under leaves, he even dipped his paws into the cold water, but he could not find the stick anywhere. Wrapper was terribly upset. He looked around at the fox, who was still rolling in the grass. The cub was on its back again, wagging its bushy tail, and between two little front paws, was the stick.

Wrapper's ears pricked up in relief. As he hopped over, the fox rolled onto its front, stick in mouth, tail sweeping excitedly over the ground behind. Wrapper reached forward for the stick but the fox did not let go.

Instead, it raised its fuzzy behind into the air, tail wagging furiously. "Play! Play, play, play!" squeaked the little fox, tugging at the stick. Wrapper pulled back. The two of them tugged and pulled, tugged and pulled, tugged and pulled. Eventually, the cub tugged, and Wrapper let go, falling backward onto his fluffy bottom.

He looked down at the ground, ears low, defeated, disappointed, and thoroughly upset. He gave a big sob. The cub dropped the stick and tilted its head in concern. Padding over to Wrapper, the fox nuzzled its face into the rabbit's cheek.

Despite all the warnings, Wrapper nuzzled back. "Thank you," he murmured to the cub, drying his eyes.

"Is okay," replied the fox, "What wrong?"

Wrapper looked at the cub, whom he couldn't help but trust. "I've been so excited about coming here with Grandrabbit for so long, and it's all gone wrong. I just wanted to see Grandrabbit smile. Instead, he's forgotten everything and it's all my fault. If I had listened to him, this wouldn't have happened. He doesn't like foxes you see."

The fox cub looked confused, "Me fox?"

Wrapper raised his head. "You are. Didn't you know?"

The fox shook its furry head until its ears started flapping. "There were other, bigger me's, but then I roll off. Then I chase a flappy thing," he giggled. "Then I come here." With a scratch, the cub added, "Me Ernest." He proceeded to pounce on a passing grasshopper, and then gobbled up some juicy berries from a bush.

"Well Ernest, it was nice to meet you, but I need to go and help Grandrabbit. Please can I have his stick back?"

Ernest grabbed the stick and, with an excited look and an eagerly wagging tail, said, "I come! I help!" Wrapper was unsure but agreed. After all, they might need all the help they could get.

They soon found Bea frantically running up and

down the water's edge, looking desperately through the bushes. When she spotted Wrapper, she started yelling. "Oh, I'm so sorry, I've lost him! He sat down for a rest, but I turned around and now I can't find him!"

"What? What do you mean?"

"Your Grandrabbit, he's gone!"

A cold terror fell over Wrapper.

He sat at the edge of the pond, wondering what to do. Bea had stopped her panicked hopping and was watching Ernest. The cub seemed to be no danger and was more interested in playing. His nose was lowered, sniffing as he went. After a minute of smelling, the fox pounced. When his head came up, he was holding a shiny brown frog gently in his mouth. The frog squirmed and managed to wiggle its way out, landing in the pond with a plop. The fox stared after it, ear cocked in confusion.

This gave Bea an idea. She picked up Grandrabbit's stick and went over to the fox. Wrapper watched as she offered it to Ernest. He sniffed, lifted his nose, wagged his tail and pounced on Wrapper, licking his face. Wrapper pushed him off and the cub rolled away.

"What was that?" he asked Bea.

"He could smell the frog! Maybe he can smell your Grandrabbit?"

Wrapper looked thoughtful; it was a good idea.

Bea offered the stick to Ernest again. Looking at him, she said, "Smell more." Concentrating, the fox sniffed. After a few good sniffs he jumped up and snatched the stick from Bea. Without a word, he went running off through the bushes. "Follow him, quick!"

They desperately wanted to find Grandrabbit. The cub had disappeared out of sight over the brow of a hill, and as the two rabbits came over the crest, they saw Ernest's tail wagging furiously. They drew nearer and saw a big dusty crater opening up before them. As they joined him at the edge, they saw that the bottom was littered with old leaves, twigs and seeds. There, sitting hunched, closed eyed and shivering, was Grandrabbit.

Wrapper felt so relieved, and called out to his Grandrabbit. He did not respond. Not even a twitch of an ear. "Grandrabbit! Grandrabbit!"

Bea joined in, "Grandrabbit! Grandrabbit! GRANDRABBIT!" The old grey rabbit looked up, with confused eyes.

Wrapper reached out, "Take my paw, we need to go home."

Grandrabbit shook his head, frightened. "Where am I?" came his shaky voice. His eyes slid from the rabbits he no longer recognised, to the fox cub looking down at him innocently. "My stick!" exclaimed Grandrabbit, as he saw what the fox was carrying, "That's my walking stick!" He hopped over frailly and struggled to reach the stick.

"Ernest, lean over! Let him hold the stick, and pull with all your strength!" Bea ordered. So that's exactly what he did. Grandrabbit jumped up, reaching with his paw. He missed, hopped, missed, hopped, missed. Ernest stretched. Grandrabbit finally managed to grab the end, where he dangled feebly. The fox began to slide toward the edge of the crater. He dug his claws into the dirt, but he continued to slip. Wrapper

grabbed hold of Ernest and Bea grabbed Wrapper. They pulled, and they pulled, and they pulled. Eventually, Grandrabbit's grey ears appeared, followed by his fluffy head, and finally, his damp, exhausted body. They all collapsed in a heap, panting.

Once they had caught their breath, Wrapper hopped to Grandrabbit's side.

"I'm so sorry, Grandrabbit," he said, as he snuggled deep into the old rabbit's fur.

"It's okay Wrapper," he said, squeezing his grandson to him. Wrapper breathed a heavy sigh of relief; he could remember!

Ernest led the way back down the hill towards the pond, tail wagging, head held high, walking stick carried proudly in his mouth. Wrapper and Bea each held one of Grandrabbit's paws, supporting him as they went. They stopped for a rest when they got to the water and tucked into Bea's dandelions. Ernest dropped the stick at Grandrabbit's feet.

As the rabbit picked it up, he looked at the cub thoughtfully. "You know, I thought I'd seen everything in my long years. I thought I knew all there was to know. Today, little cub, you have proved me wrong. I shouldn't have mistrusted you." The old rabbit reached out a paw. Ernest licked Grandrabbit's cheek and rolled over, tongue lolling.

When the dandelions were all gone, the three rabbits stood up to leave.

Ernest however, stayed sitting. "I stay, I like here," said the cub.

Grandrabbit smiled and nodded, "Good, I'm very glad you like it."

The fox sneezed as he smiled back.

"Can we come back and play with you soon?" asked Wrapper.

"Yes, and I come play too?"

"You can have a go on our swing!" replied Bea enthusiastically.

As the rabbits hopped away, they left the fluffy little cub happily chasing a crispy brown leaf blowing in the breeze, pouncing on it with a satisfying crunch.

Wrapper and Bea held Grandrabbit's paw all the way back to Bunny Hill. As soon as they got home, Grandrabbit was quickly ushered in by Wrapper's parents and fell straight to sleep. Wrapper hoped he was okay. He had been terribly cold for a frightfully long time and was awfully tired.

Later that day, as the sun was setting, Wrapper was sitting on the swing below the Old Oak. His heart skipped, as he spotted a pair of familiar grey ears hobbling slowly toward him.

Grandrabbit was once again leaning on his walking stick, and he smiled as he got nearer, as Wrapper leapt off his seat in delight.

"Hello squire, are you okay? I'm sorry I scared you." They touched noses, Grandrabbit giving Wrapper a big hug, who squeezed back.

"Oh no Grandrabbit, it's not your fault you forgot!"

The two rabbits sat on the hillside, happily watching the orange sun setting over the valley, tree tops glistening red and gold. "Can we have another day out soon please?"

His Grandrabbit smiled down at him, "I would like that." Wrapper looked up at his Grandrabbit, whom he loved very much.

The Bravery of Bea

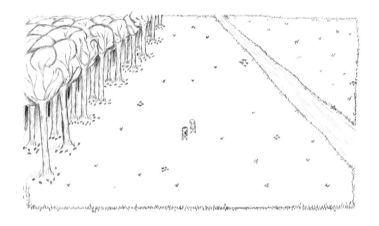

Autumn had truly taken hold of Scotney Castle. The leaves were falling fast, and what was once luscious green was now brown and barren. The warm days of the summer seemed far behind them. On this particular afternoon, the sky was a light grey, with the sun occasionally peeking through the clouds. The air was cool, although the wind had gone elsewhere.

Wrapper and Bea had been feeling adventurous when they awoke and had decided to cross the river. In fact, they had been so brave that they had ventured far across the open grassland which lay beyond. They merrily skipped their way through the fields, keeping the river to their left and the Kilndown woods looming over them ominously on their right.

Eventually, they came across a trail that led up and out of sight below the trees. However, the rabbits certainly had no intention of visiting the forest ever again; they knew just how tricky it could be there! Instead, the two friends decided to stop where they found themselves and graze for a little while.

Wrapper was rummaging near the woodlands edge when he spotted a funny looking something growing from the old mossy stump of a fallen tree. He gave the shiny brown things a tentative sniff. It smelt earthy, and Wrapper was just about to take a small bite, when he heard Bea calling from across the grass.

"Wrapper come quick, look what I've found!"

He hopped over as fast as his legs would take him, and found the fluffy brown rabbit standing proudly over a patch of sunshine yellow flowers. Her cream-coloured tail wagged happily, as Wrapper's eyes widened. Dandelions! Wrapper's absolute favourite. These flowers had slowly been disappearing from Bunny Hill, until eventually they had all vanished. Bea knew how much her friend liked dandelions and had been keeping an eye out for some all day.

Wrapper began to wolf them down greedily, Bea

helping herself to a couple. When they had finished the last of the dandelions, they looked around them, bellies significantly fuller. Noticing a small gap in the thorny bushes that grew along the riverbank, they decided to take a closer look. What they found was a small, tired looking, wooden bridge.

Without hesitation Wrapper put a paw up onto the bridge and hopped on. Walking forward with care, he made his way over. It creaked a little as he went, but held his weight and he was soon across.

"It's safe," he called back to Bea, who had not followed immediately, choosing to watch from the safety of the bank. She wasn't sure, but trusted her friend.

Tentatively, she hopped lightly onto the bridge. It creaked menacingly as she slowly made her way across. Bea peaked over the edge. The water seemed to swirl angrily below. Her heart began to beat faster as she felt how slippery the wood was under her paws. She began to shake. Her back legs scrabbled behind her wildly in panic as she tried to push herself forward. Eventually, Bea flopped off the other side, panting.

Wrapper stood looking at her, amused. "Well, you fluffed that up didn't you!" He grinned cheekily and ran off laughing.

Bea trembled as she caught her breath. She was

thoroughly annoyed at Wrapper. The bridge was jolly scary, and he had not warned her that it was wet. Not only that, but he had laughed at her, which hurt most of all.

Bea pulled herself up and joined her friend, looking cross. Even Wrapper could see something was wrong, however he presumed that she was just cross at herself, so he began to look around. The grass was a little longer here. As he was nuzzling through, he came across yet another of the funny looking things that he had seen growing on the tree stump. However, this one was a little different, and stood slightly wonky, with a little red cap. Wrapper felt the temptation growing inside of him.

"What are you looking at?" came Bea's sharp voice. He jumped around and her eyes landed on the grass behind him. "You're not going to eat that are you?" Wrapper puffed himself up.

"Maybe I am," he said defensively, noticing the tone in her voice.

"Wrapper, you mustn't, that's a mushroom, they're bad for rabbits!" she replied.

"Says who?"

"It's a bad idea"

"Don't be a scaredy-hop."

"You're being stupid," and with that she turned tail and stropped off.

Well, Wrapper did not appreciate being spoken to like that. He looked back at the mushroom. Wrapper thought for a moment, and took a small, defiant bite.

A little while later the two sat under a tall tree, a thick, sulky silence in the air, their backs turned. Neither had spoken for some time. They had not fought before and were not enjoying it. Wrapper could feel the mushroom sitting in his stomach. The red cap had left a strange, bitter taste at the back of his mouth. It had not been particularly easy to eat either and had needed much chewing. He had managed to force it down however, although as his ears grew hot and the tree in front of him swayed a little, Wrapper started to wonder whether it had been a good idea after all.

Wrapper's tummy suddenly gave a little gurgle.

"Pardon," said Bea shortly, twitching an ear in Wrapper's direction.

"Nothing," he responded icily, as he looked down at his stomach with growing concern. Moments later, his tummy gave a second, louder gurgle.

"What are you saying?" said Bea crossly.

"Nothing!" Wrapper snapped back again. Bea glared at him disbelievingly. "Maybe we should go home," he added.

"Fine" she said, standing up abruptly. Bea began to hop back toward the bridge and Wrapper followed, tummy grumbling at him as he went.

As Bea approached the bridge, she had a look of fierce determination in her eye. She hopped up onto the old wooden bridge, and made her way over, looking straight ahead, never slowing or stopping. She hopped off the other side and turned around proudly. As she looked back, Bea watched her friend climb up and begin to hop across. The brown rabbit noticed that Wrapper was moving slowly and awkwardly. He stopped in the middle of the bridge, slouching to his belly. Despite her irritation, she felt a twinge of concern.

"Are you alright?" she called from the safety of the riverbank. Wrapper nodded. He tried to stand up, but fell straight back down. Bea jumped back onto the bridge.

"Wrapper, what's wrong?" she asked again.

"My tummy aches," he admitted this time. "I just need to lay here for a few minutes." As he spoke, the bridge gave an ominous creak. Bea looked down at the bridge nervously. As she took another step, a loud cracking came from beneath their paws. Bea jumped, but Wrapper didn't move.

"We can't stay here!" she said, her voice fearful. Wrapper dragged himself to his feet and began to pull himself forward.

More cracking sounds came from the bridge. Her heart was racing as Wrapper slowly crawled across. *Too slow*, she thought, *they wouldn't make it*. Thinking fast, she hopped around Wrapper, coming perilously close to the slippery edge. Once behind, she pushed on his back end, sliding him forward, yet more cracking coming from below. Eventually, Wrapper fell off the other side. Bea leapt after him, just as a great snapping came from the bridge. Splintered wood crashed into the river below.

Bea looked back in shock. Her chest felt tight and she was struggling to breathe. Wrapper wobbled to his feet and stumbled out into the field beyond. As she emerged into the grass, she found him lying on his back, paws in the air, staring up at the sky.

"I feel funny," he said as she approached. "My head feels all wobbly and my tummy isn't right."

Bea did not like the sound of that one bit. "Come on, let's get you home," she said firmly. Wrapper rolled back onto his front. He wobbled as he stood up, clutching at his stomach, moving unsteadily forward. "Here," said Bea begrudgingly, offering him a paw. He took it gratefully, leaning heavily on her.

Step by step, they made their way back in the direction of Bunny Hill. They were just crossing the top of a large slope, high up from the river, when Wrapper stopped.

"Uh-oh," he said, as he clutched his stomach and

screwed up his fluffy face. He dropped to the floor in pain, and the steep slope sent him rolling away.

"Wrapper!" Bea shouted in a panic, as he disappeared out of sight. She hopped after him as fast as she could, and found Wrapper laid amongst a patch of tall, tough grass, half submerged in mud. His ears were low, he was covered in dirt and looked desperately sorry for himself.

He looked up at her through unfocused eyes.

"I'm so sorry Bea. I shouldn't have eaten that mushroom."

She blinked at him in disbelief. "Why would you eat that? I told you not to!"

"I know, I should have listened." He wrinkled his face up in pain. "I thought you were just saying that because you were annoyed at fluffing up crossing the bridge." Despite her best friend's great discomfort, Bea felt a flash of irritation.

"I was annoyed because you laughed at me, Wrapper!" The muddy rabbit looked most surprised by this. Bea continued, "I was scared. I needed you to be a good friend, not just run off and leave me." Wrapper felt terrible. Bea had always been a good friend to him, no matter what the situation.

"I'm sorry," he hung his head in shame.

Bea could see that he meant it, and felt the weight of anger lift from her shoulders and float away. She squeezed Wrapper's paw and smiled. "Let's get you out of here." Bea pulled, and with a great squelching sound, Wrapper was freed from the mud.

Once back on the trail, Bea looked at Wrapper. His paw was not leaving his tummy, and his eyes were wide, yet unseeing. He wobbled so much when he walked that she could barely keep him upright. Bea was frightened, but led the way. As she supported her friend, she could feel him growing weaker and weaker, moving slower and slower.

They had been walking for what seemed a very long time, when Wrapper slumped. He fell to the floor, legs giving way beneath him, ears limp. Bea fell with him, and found herself laying in squelchy, wet mud.

She shook Wrapper, who's eyes were closed. "Wake up!"

He murmured, the noise barely escaping his mouth, but no words formed.

Bea felt desperate. She looked around her wildly through shimmering eyes, and caught sight of the Old Castle from across the river. She had never seen it before. The old stone was cracked and  crumbling, with ivy growing up its stained walls. The castle was surrounded by a shimmering moat, which itself was surrounded by beautiful gardens. This place was said to be magic. Or at least, that's what Grandrabbit had told them.

She stared, for a moment lost in wonder. As she gazed, a strange feeling seemed to fill her heart, and a new courage spread throughout her entire body. She jumped to her feet and gritted her teeth, gathering all her remaining strength.

"Right," she said with a newfound determination, "I can do this! Come on, we're going to get you home." She began to move once more, half carrying, half shoving Wrapper along as they went, refusing to give up.

Bea pushed, pulled, nudged, and rolled her best friend through the grass. The black and white rabbit's eyes were closed fast, and he grew muddier and muddier as they went. Bea was exhausted, as if she too may collapse at any minute. As she felt her legs starting to shake beneath her, she heard a familiar sound ahead of her. *Tap-Tap-Tap-Tap*.

She looked up. *Tap-Tap-Tap-Tap*. Her heart skipped, "Walter!" she called out desperately. "Walter, are you there?"

The green bird with a red head landed on a small rock just ahead. *Tap-Tap-Tap-Tap*. "Bea! What's happened?" he asked with great concern as he took in the scene before him.

"Wrapper's eaten something bad, he's terribly ill."

"Oh no!" *TAP-TAP-TAP-TAP*. "What are we going to do!" *TAP-TAP-TAP-TAP*.

"Go and get Clarence, now! Tell him to come quick!"

TAP-TAP-TAP-TAP. With a nod, Walter flew off as quickly as his wings would flap.

Bea continued to struggle through the grass. A little while later, came the sound of loud hooves from across the field, as two curled horns appeared on the horizon.

"I see you've managed to wake me up again," grumbled the big brown cow. He stopped, and his eyes widened below his long fringe as he caught sight of the limp rabbit in Bea's tired arms. "My goodness! What in Scotney did he eat?" Clarence exclaimed with alarm.

TAP-TAP-TAP-TAP, went Walter.

"A mushroom sir," explained Bea, "please help him."

Clarence gulped, growing ever more concerned. "We must get him home, quickly." The cow knelt down in front of the two rabbits. "Climb on, I'll carry you both the rest of the way."

Bea struggled to get Wrapper up onto Clarence's back. She pushed and shoved at her friend, Walter tapping anxiously all the while. Finally, she managed to get her shoulder under him, and heaved him up onto the cow. She hopped up after him, only just managing in her exhaustion. Clarence rose to his feet. Wrapper started to slip, and Bea reached forward to grab her friend.

"Make sure you hold him tight," he said as he began to move forward, as fast as he could whilst keeping them both safely on his back. Bea held Wrapper fast to her as they went.

The large brown cow carried them a long way, as Walter flapped alongside. They passed through the patch of trees that the woodpecker and cow called home, and gave Mrs Woollencot quite the fright as they crossed the large stone bridge back over the river. She had been happily grazing on the other side, and had definitely not been expecting to see a cow with two sorry looking rabbits on its back come trotting quickly across, followed by a worried woodpecker. She stared as they passed, bewildered.

They crossed the stream, back onto Bunny Hill. The other rabbits looked just as surprised as the sheep had, some even running for their burrows.

Bea shouted desperately, "Has anyone seen Mr Muddypaw?" She was looking for Wrapper's dad, who she knew would know just what to do.

"Up that way!" shouted a big grey rabbit, pointing toward the west end of the village, "near the beehives." Clarence didn't need telling twice. He began up the hill in the direction the rabbit had pointed, his big hooves slipping in the wet grass as he went.

As they drew near the beehives, Bea caught sight of Wrapper's dad and called out "Mr Muddypaw! Mr Muddypaw!"

He turned at the sound of his name. As soon as he saw his son laying lifeless on the cows back, he came hopping quickly over. "Bea what has happened?" he asked urgently.

"He ate a mushroom sir, with a red hat. I got him here as fast as I could, I promise!"

Mr Muddypaw took a deep breath as he looked at Wrapper. "We need to get him home, now. This way!" he said, hopping off in the direction of their burrow, beckoning for the cow to follow. "Bea, bring me some water."

She watched desperately as her friend disappeared.

A long while later, when it was almost dark, Bea found herself sitting outside Wrapper's burrow with a concerned looking cow and a still tapping woodpecker. Eventually, they heard footsteps coming from down the tunnel, and all three faces turned. Out hopped Wrapper's dad.

"Mr Muddypaw, is he okay?" she asked nervously.

He looked at all three of their anxious faces, and broke into a smile. "Yes, the mushroom is leaving his body. He still feels a little poorly, but he's going to be fine." The relief in his eyes was clear to see. "Thank you all so much," he continued "you got him here just in time." He turned to Bea, "would you like to come and see him?"

Bea hopped down the tunnel, following Mr Muddypaw. After a few twists and turns, Wrapper came into sight. He looked exhausted and was still rubbing his tummy a little, but his eyes no longer seemed to look without seeing. Mr Muddypaw gave Bea a grateful pat on the back before he hopped away. They looked at each other for a moment. Then Bea threw herself at

Wrapper, giving him a big hug. Wrapper hugged back, wincing a little. He smiled up at Bea as she pulled away.

She blinked at him.

"I'm sorry you ate that mushroom because of me," she said, guiltily. "I shouldn't have been so cross."

Wrapper stared at her in shock. "Don't be so silly. It was my choice."

"But if I'd said it nicely…"

"I would probably have eaten it anyway. And besides, it was me that was the bad friend."

Bea looked at him. "Next time we get annoyed, we should talk about it. Not fight with each other."

Wrapper nodded in agreement, "That sounds like a much better idea to me."

The two rabbits touched noses and knew that they would always be best friends.

The Old Tale

Heavy rain drops poured down from a dark grey sky, the bare branches of autumn creaking and moaning in the fierce wind. The stream flowed swiftly at the foot of Bunny Hill, as water ran off the grassy slope. Wrapper stared out miserably from a warm, dry burrow.

"It's not going to stop, is it?" he said glumly, ears drooping.

"I don't think it is, no," Bea replied.

Wrapper sighed, "Fine. What shall we do then?" The two rabbits were huddled together in the entrance to

Bea's burrow, watching the storm sweep through the valley. They were spending the day together and had planned to go exploring across the river again. However, when Wrapper woke up, he had found a grey drizzle already in the air, and a stiff breeze blowing across the hillside. By the time he had reached Bea, the dark clouds had opened and Wrapper was sopping wet.

He had almost dried now, but the downpour was far from over.

"We'll just have to stay here I suppose. We can play games?" Bea suggested.

Wrapper thought for a moment. "We could play make believe?"

Bea nodded enthusiastically, "Yes! Where shall we go today?"

Wrapper puffed up his chest, standing in a brave rabbit stance. "Today, Bea, we will be climbing the biggest, scariest, most tallest mountain in the world."

Bea shivered with excitement, "Okay, Captain Wrapper, where do we begin?"

"First, we must find the mountain. Follow me, Captain Bea, adventure awaits!" Wrapper bounced off down the tunnel.

Bea stopped as they reached the living room. "Look Wrapper, there it is," she said with awe.

Wrapper's eyes widened. "It's so beautiful." The two rabbits stared in amazement, as they took in the glorious mountain before them. This was in fact, the armchair, bookcase and small table that sat in the corner of the room.

Bea stepped forward boldly. "I shall now begin the climb." She hopped toward the armchair, and with a big jump, leapt up.

Wrapper, standing at the foot of the chair, watched her disappear out of sight. "Captain Bea, what do you see?"

"Oh Wrapper, it's amazing. There's a big blue lake with great golden fish in it." Her head appeared over the edge of the cushion, peering down at him. "Are you going to make it up?"

"Yes, I think I can do it." His tail gave a little wiggle, and Wrapper hopped up to join Bea.

The two rabbits gazed around them.

"Do you see a path up?" asked Bea.

"I think so, look." He twitched his ear toward the arm of the chair. "We use this foothill, and then scramble up that large rock. From there, we might be able to make it to the very top." Wrapper eyed the bookcase keenly.

Bea gulped. The way up seemed a little risky. "Captain

Wrapper, I do not wish to fall off the mountain…. also, I don't want to break any of my mum's things."

Wrapper grinned at her. "Only the bravest will triumph." He slicked back his ears and prepared for the ascent.

He leapt into action. The arm of the chair was easy enough, and Wrapper made it with a single hop. The climb up the large rock was more of a challenge. One hop took him half way, scrabbling desperately with his paws to make the rest. Once he was up, he sat on the back of the armchair, catching his breath. "Bea, you look so tiny from up here!" he called down to the brown rabbit.

She looked up, uncertain. "Wrapper… are you sure this is a good idea?"

Without responding, Wrapper leapt from the chair. He stretched out hopefully for the mountain top. His front paws grabbed the top of the bookcase… but the rest of him didn't quite make it. He hung on desperately. The bookcase began to wobble. Bea watched with horror as it

toppled forward and crashed noisily to the floor, books flying everywhere.

"What was that?" came an angry voice from somewhere down the burrow.

"Ohhh. No, no, no, Wrapper, what have you done?" Bea said in a terrified whisper. She hopped back and forth around the scattered pile of books, wringing her ears nervously. Wrapper's head popped up from beneath a large book, looking rather shocked.

"I think I fell off the mountain."

Bea's mum burst into the room. "Beatrice Wiggletail, what is going on?" she demanded, as she took in the two guilty looking rabbits staring up at her. Wrapper's ears sunk low, but Bea sat up tall.

"I'm sorry mum, we were playing make believe and trying to climb a mountain…. it's raining outside."

"I see," she said, arms crossed. Her fur was the same brown as that of her daughter. "Well, I think you had better tidy this up," looking around at the books scattered across the room, "and then we'll see if we can't find something to keep you two out of trouble."

Wrapper and Bea began tidying up the mess their adventure had resulted in. They righted the bookcase and started re-stacking the shelves with its large collection of books.

"Bea, why does your mum have so many books?" he asked curiously as he examined the colourful covers.

"She just really likes reading. She reads to me a lot too. It's good for you!"

Wrapper nodded in agreement; his family would read him bedtime stories almost every night. He picked up a book with an old drawing of a white rabbit on the cover. "Has she read all of these books?"

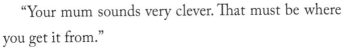

"I don't know, I think so! She's a professor you see."

"What's a professor?"

"She knows lots of things and teaches people!"

"Your mum sounds very clever. That must be where you get it from."

Bea smiled proudly. "I hope I can be as smart as mum one day."

A short while later, the books were all returned to their shelves, in almost the right order. Bea's mother, who's full title was Professor Katie Wiggletail, came into the room.

She looked around. "Okay, that's better," she concluded, once she had accounted for every book.

"Sorry mum," said Bea again.

"Sorry Mrs Wiggletail," Wrapper added.

"It's okay you two, I know you were just having fun. But try not to do it again, alright?" The two young rabbits nodded their heads vigorously in agreement. "Now, what shall we do for the rest of the day?" She looked back at the bookcase. "How about a story?"

"Oh yes please!" said Bea, tail wiggling excitedly.

"Can we have an adventure story? Please?" added Wrapper quickly, ears raised.

The professor smiled at them. "How about I tell you the greatest tale of all?"

"Yay! A make-believe story!"

"Oh no, my dear Wrapper. The greatest stories of all, are true." She reached up, and pulled an old, weathered looking book from the top shelf.

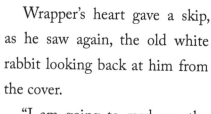

Wrapper's heart gave a skip, as he saw again, the old white rabbit looking back at him from the cover.

"I am going to read you the story of the Great White Rabbit. Without him, none of us would be here today." Professor Katie Wiggletail settled herself down in her armchair and picked up her reading glasses from the small table next to her. She looked down at the two rabbits sitting cross-legged in front of her, staring up in anticipation. "Are we sitting comfortably? Good, then I shall begin."

"A long, long time ago, in a land not too far away from here, rabbits stretched as far as the eye could see. They lived happily together, over the rolling hills, amongst the ancient trees and even as far away as the great blueness at the very edge of the world. All was peaceful, until one day a shadow fell upon the land, when the ones that walk tall came from across the water."

Bea shuddered, "The humans?" she asked in a whisper, and her mum nodded. Wrapper gulped. Even he knew about humans, although luckily, he had never seen one.

"As soon as they arrived, the humans began chopping down trees, churning up fields, and destroying our homes. The rabbits were left scattered, and terrified of what the humans might do next. Until one day, a hero appeared. One by one, a great white rabbit bravely hopped across the lands, uniting the rabbits together once more. Nobody knew where he came from. All they knew was his name; Oriktus."

"That's a very strange name," observed Wrapper.

"He was a very strange rabbit," agreed the professor, "for he had little fear of humans." She continued, "Once Oriktus had gathered all the rabbits he could find, he began to lead them across the ruined world of the tall ones, crossing their stone fields, over great scars in the earth and through poisoned rivers, all the while keeping his people safe."

"The humans were hunting them down, and were never far behind, destroying everything in their path. Day by day, night by night, the Great White Rabbit

led his rabbits onward. One day, they reached the edge of a frightfully large forest. The trees were so thick, that they could not see beyond the treeline. As they looked, unsure of what to do, they heard the racket of the humans behind them, nearer than ever. In that moment, Oriktus knew what he must do. He turned his back on the destruction of the humans and pointed his nose toward the woodland. The trees suddenly seemed inviting and peaceful, and the smell of nature filled his nose, untouched by the tall ones. He hopped forward and entered the forest."

Bea gasped, "But he did not know the way! That was jolly brave!" They all knew that if a rabbit did not know their way amongst trees, they could get lost far too easily.

"Indeed. The Great White Rabbit had a courage that few possess. They could hear the sounds of the humans hacking and cutting at the trees behind them. However, the tall ones could not move freely through the forest, and soon, the world of the humans disappeared, far, far behind. As they hopped deeper and deeper into the woods, they felt the fear leaving them. They were not even scared of getting lost anymore. After all, where else were they to go?"

"Many of them chose to stop amongst the trees as they went, settling down and creating new lives within the forest. Oriktus however, did not stop. He continued his journey through the woodland. Eventually, after a terribly long time, Oriktus emerged from the trees, accompanied by a loyal band of rabbits. Before their paws, stretched a luscious green land, full of grass, waterways and patches of trees. The Great White rabbit had led his people to a new world, where they could feel safe from the tall ones for many, many years."

Wrapper and Bea stared up from the rug below the

professor's feet, mouths open in wonder.

"Where was this magical place?" asked Wrapper, with great curiosity.

"Have you not guessed yet?" Bea's mum replied, looking at him over the top of her reading glasses. She turned a page. "The Great White Rabbit knew, that somewhere amongst these fields, lay their new home. So Oriktus began to hop through the tall grass, all the way down to a rushing river."

"Too deep and too fast for them to swim, Oriktus hopped along the riverbank, until they found a great fallen ash tree. The old tree was rotten, and slippery with moss, but the white rabbit knew that this was the only way across, so he bravely jumped on and slowly crept over. The other rabbits followed. A few almost fell, but with a little luck and a lot of determination, they all made it across safely."

"They found themselves in a field full of daisies and dandelions and they hopped gleefully through. Oriktus however, was clever, and knew that this was too close to the river. He did not want to have come all this way, only for their burrows to be flooded come the first rain. Ahead of them he noticed that the ground began to slope up, onto a beautiful hillside, dotted with trees. They found a small stream at the foot of this hill, but luckily it was only a gentle trickle of water. They splashed through together, giggling as they did so."

"They hopped up the hill and stopped beneath a great oak tree, to nibble at the flowers. Finally, the Great White Rabbit felt his quest was complete and proclaimed; *Here we shall dig our burrows and build our warrens, for this is where we truly belong. This hillside will be forever safe, and no harm will come to any rabbit that calls it home.* As his people continued to eat and merrily tell tales of their adventure, the Great White Rabbit gazed out across the green fields bathed in a golden sunset. Oriktus vowed to watch over these lands forevermore." The two young rabbits looked up at the professor, hooked on her every word. She continued, "And so, the rabbits that had followed him all the way from the destruction of the humans, through the endless forest and across the great river, came to live on this hillside, and stayed there happily ever after."

Suddenly, something clicked in Wrapper's brain. He looked up at the professor in disbelief. "Is it? Could it be?" Professor Wiggletail smiled and nodded. Wrapper jumped up with excitement. "Bunny Hill! The Great White Rabbit led his people here. The oak is *the* Old Oak, the stream is the Sweetbourne, and the river is the same river we crossed!" He suddenly stopped, a look of fear dawning across his face. "And the endless trees.... are the Kilndown woods?" Bea's mum nodded again kindly. "But the tall ones are coming?" he added fearfully.

"Do not worry young rabbit. All these years later, the spirit of Oriktus still protects us. And the Woodland rabbits continue to live amongst the trees, protecting us from anything that might try to reach us." This comforted Wrapper somewhat, although he could not shake the thought of the humans, still hacking and chopping their way through.

With a thump, the professor shut the book. Wrapper jumped, chasing the tall ones from his mind.

"The End."

Bea wiggled her ears happily, "I can't believe that's a true story!"

"Well, there are some that believe it is just a myth."

"What's a myth?"

"Old stories from times long forgotten. Nobody is sure of their origins, or how true they are. Some rabbits believe them, some don't."

Wrapper frowned, "Then how do you know it is true?"

"The story of Oriktus has been passed down from mother to daughter, father to son, generation to generation, all the way from when the first rabbits settled on the hill. Even the rabbits of the Kilndown have old stories of the Great White Rabbit. And from time to time, the white rabbit can still be seen hopping through the fields and amongst the trees. Once you have seen him, you know his story to be true." The professor smiled a knowing smile, laid the book on the table, rested her glasses on top and rose from her chair. She left the two rabbits sitting in stunned silence.

After a while, Bea looked at Wrapper, "So, did you enjoy the story?" He looked back at her but did not reply. "Wrapper, are you okay?" A strange, thoughtful expression had come over his face.

Eventually, he said in a voice little more than a whisper, "Bea, your mum said that the rabbits lived here happily forever. And that the story was passed down, parent to child, all the way from the first rabbits of the hill."

"She did," Bea agreed in mild confusion, "I was listening too."

Wrapper seemed to be quivering slightly, like a coiled spring. "Do you not realise what that means?"

She thought for a minute. Eventually, she asked curiously, "What?"

"It means…it means…oh Bea, it means…"

"What Wrapper? What does it mean?"

The spring sprung and Wrapper jumped up, whizzing around the room.

"We are the rabbits of Oriktus!" His voice was loud and excited as he continued to run laps around his friend. "Our Grandrabbit's, Grandrabbit's, Grandrabbit's, Grandrabbit's, Grandrabbit's, Grandrabbit's, Grandrabbit's were the ones who followed Oriktus all the way through the endless forest."

Bea was smiling and laughing at her friend's excitement, "I take it you believe the story of the White Rabbit then?"

"Oh yes! I hope I get to meet him one day!"

"Hmm, I'm not sure, that sounds a little scary to me Wrapper," she replied, but he was too busy being excited to hear her.

"We should play! Let's pretend to be heroes, just like those first rabbits, and follow Oriktus on an adventure!"

As he said this, he bumped into the bookcase, which wobbled. They both stared up at it in terror.

The bookcase settled and its books remained in place. The two rabbits both let out a relieved sigh.

Bea looked at Wrapper, and with a nervous laugh, said, "Okay, we'll go on an adventure with the Great White Rabbit, but maybe not in here! Let me go and see if it's still raining." She hopped up the tunnel, leaving Wrapper dreaming of adventures.

"Oh look, come quickly!" came Bea's voice from up the tunnel. He hopped toward her and found her standing in the entrance of the burrow. The rain had cleared, and the clouds were scattered. They had left behind a brilliant blue sky, the sun shining brightly. The light glittered off the wet grass, as a rainbow danced through the air. Wrapper's fur stood on end as he felt the spirit of the white rabbit all around them.

The Lost Acorn

It was a cold autumn afternoon, the wind whistling through the trees of Scotney Castle. As the last few leaves desperately clung to their branches, spikey conkers and chestnut shells rained down from above. The ground felt muddy save for crispy brown leaves, which crunched satisfyingly under foot. Nonetheless, every so often the sun poked its head from behind the clouds, making the grass sparkle below.

Today, Wrapper found himself a little to the north of Bunny Hill, accompanied by his best friend Bea and his newest friend, Ernest the fox cub. They were merrily grazing amongst the damp grass, snuffling up any discarded berries or other tasty treats that may have been missed. Every so often Ernest would lift his shiny black nose to the sky, keenly sniffing the air. Whenever he caught the scent of something in the distance, the young fox would go bouncing off eagerly in pursuit, re-appearing a short while later.

A silvery mist hung loosely in the air as they drew close to the edge of the nearby woodland. Wrapper caught sight of something amongst the grass.

"What's that over there?" The other two lifted their heads and stared in the direction that the black and white rabbit was indicating.

"What, Wrapper? I don't see anything." replied the brown furred Bea. Ernest cocked his orange fluffy head in confusion. Wrapper hopped nearer and what he saw filled him with curiosity. Close to the treeline, beneath the outer branches that loomed overhead, was a wide, intriguing ring, of exceedingly large toadstools. They were so big that Wrapper felt sure that he could quite comfortably sit on one!

The others arrived just behind him. Bea stopped and stared in wonder.

"Oooh," she gasped, "how wonderful." She reached out a fluffy paw to touch one of the great toadstools.

Ernest suddenly dropped to his front paws and growled ominously, hackles raised, and Bea pulled her paw away instinctively.

"What is it? What's wrong?" asked Wrapper quickly.

"Something," Ernest replied, unhelpfully, staring straight ahead intently. The two rabbits had never seen the cub like this before. He was usually so bouncy, that it was a struggle to get him to do anything other than play.

Wrapper and Bea sat down and looked at the arrangement before them.

"It could be magic," Bea said after some silence.

"Could it?" Wrapper said in surprise.

"Maybe, mum told me that fairies live in these woods, and that they only come out for special occasions."

Wrapper believed in magic, of course, but he had never heard of any fairies living in the valley, save in the castle gardens. Bea was usually right however, so he supposed it must be true. "Maybe this is the work fairies then. Why else would they grow like that?" Wrapper suddenly felt a jolt of excitement. "Bea, what if there's a fairy in there right now, hiding?"

"It could be possible!" she said staring into the fairy ring.

"What else did your mum tell you about fairies?"

"Well," Bea began thoughtfully, "I know they like chestnuts. Sometimes we leave them out as presents!"

"Perfect!" Wrapper jumped up in glee, "Then let's go and find some." He hopped off amongst the trees in search of these scrumptious fairy treats.

Bea looked at the fluffy cub still staring into the fairy ring. "Ernest, stay here and keep watch."

The fox did not blink.

A short time later, the rabbits came running back, each holding a fresh chestnut tightly in their paws. When they reached the fairy ring, they found Ernest exactly where they had left him, still lying flat in the grass. As they approached, the fox began to growl once again, but he did not try to stop them. Wrapper and Bea crossed the threshold, and entered the fairy ring.

The air inside seemed to stand still. The noises of the woods around them became dull in their keen ears. They even felt a slight tingling in their paws and Wrapper's tail stood on end. He looked over at Bea, who nodded meaningfully at him. *Yes*, thought Wrapper with nervous excitement, *there is definitely magic here*. As they reached the centre, they both delicately placed their chestnuts down into the soft grass and took a few steps back, waiting.

Nothing happened. Wrapper felt disappointed. Or

maybe it was hunger. Either way, he did not like it. He felt Bea take his paw.

"It's okay," she said, seeing the obvious upset on his face, "Maybe it's just shy. They might come out if we hop away." Dejected, Wrapper turned his back on the chestnuts, and the two rabbits left the ring of toadstools. As they began to hop off back through the grass, they heard Ernest let out a short, sharp, bark. The two rabbits span around.

There, standing in the middle of the fairy ring, chestnut in hand, nibbling delightfully away.... was a squirrel.

"Hey!" Wrapper shouted at the squirrel, annoyed, "They're not for you!"

The squirrel dropped the chestnut and looked up in surprise, then asked urgently, "Have you seen my acorn?"

"Your acorn?" Bea replied in bewilderment.

"Yes, my acorn. I can't find it and its very important!" The squirrel skipped through the grass toward them. Whilst decidedly not a fairy, it was still rather unusual and looked remarkably different from all of the other squirrels living in Scotney Castle. For one, Wrapper thought it was a little smaller, and it also had large tufts of hair growing up from its pointed ears. Most notably however, this squirrel, rather than the usual grey, was as red as the setting sun.

The red squirrel hopped around erratically amongst the grass. "My acorn," he kept repeating to himself agitatedly, not really paying attention to the confused rabbits staring at him, "Where-oh-where is my acorn?"

"That fairy?" asked Ernest curiously.

"No, that's a squirrel," explained Bea, and the cub wagged his tail. "Although I've never seen one that colour," she said with intrigue, looking at Wrapper.

He shook his head in response, then turned to the squirrel. "Did you need some help?" he asked, as the squirrel continued to search frantically. Wrapper looked a little closer, and noticed that the rich, red fur seemed to have a silvery grey haze to it. He concluded that the squirrel must be quite old, although he moved as freely as a feather on the wind.

"Oh yes please, young rabbit, that would be most

gracious!" he paused for a moment, "Pray, what are your names?" he asked politely.

"This is Bea, and this is Ernest," Wrapper said, indicating his two friends, "And my name is Wrapper. What's yours?"

"My name is Cecil, I'm so pleased to meet you," his eyes continuing to dart around as he spoke.

"Cecil," said Bea, "why is this acorn so important to you?"

"The cold is coming," he said to her in a serious tone, "and I must gather as much food as I can before it does." He looked up at the bare trees above in concern. "But time is short... it is almost here." As he spoke, the wind let out a great breath, sending leaves fluttering ominously to the ground.

"I must have dropped it somewhere on my way home," Cecil continued.

"Where's home, Cecil?" enquired Bea.

"Why, right here of course", he said, waving toward the ring of toadstools.

"You live in a ring of toad stools?" said Wrapper, doubtfully.

"Don't be daft! Can you not see the tree?" replied the squirrel, confidently.

A sudden understanding came over Wrapper. As

Cecil stared up at a tree that only he could see, Wrapper wondered if, like his Grandrabbit, the squirrel had grown a little confused in his old age. Wrapper, giving Bea a meaningful look and knowing exactly what to do, smiled kindly at Cecil. "Okay, let's find your acorn, shall we?"

Cecil sat up tall on his back legs, "Yes, on the double!"

"Can you remember where you last had it?"

Cecil shook his head. "I had just curled up for a nice nap when I realised the acorn was missing, but many leaves have fallen since then."

Ernest slowly approached the squirrel, hackles lowered for the first time, and gave his silvery red fur a few, tentative sniffs. As the wind blew once more, the fox cub's nosed twitched keenly, and he raced off into the woods.

"Ah yes, the fox has the right of it. Hop to it young rabbits!" he called back as he skipped assuredly after Ernest. Wrapper and Bea looked at each other, and quickly followed suit. They hoped the cub knew where he was going, but hoped even more that they might stumble upon Cecil's real home, where his family would surely be worried.

Ernest had vanished amongst the trees, but Cecil seemed to know exactly where he was going. He led the two rabbits along the small path which they knew would eventually bring them back to Bunny Hill, muttering about his acorn as they went. However, as they approached the village, he suddenly darted right through the undergrowth. Wrapper and Bea stopped.

"Are you sure this is the way?" called Bea.

"Yes," he replied with certainty.

"Do you know where you're going?" Wrapper called, full of doubt.

"No!" he shouted back, just as certainly.

Wrapper and Bea followed, and eventually found the squirrel sitting on the shore of a small lake, surface shimmering in the breeze. Cecil was looking around him, lost in thought.

"Was this where you dropped your acorn?" asked Wrapper politely.

"No," replied Cecil, softly, "this is where I met my Lillian, many, many years ago."

"Your Lillian?" asked Bea, confused. "Who's she?"

"She's the sweetest, most beautiful squirrel that ever climbed a tree. We used to scamper through the branches all day long, and snuggle up together at night, safe and warm. Lilly is my best friend, and I love her oh so much."

Bea felt a pang of sadness, although could not explain why.

"Won't she be worried about you, Cecil? Wondering where you've got to?" suggested Wrapper, tentatively.

"Oh, she went to sleep a little while ago. I will dream with her again soon." He gazed out over the lake.

"When the cold comes?"

"Yes, little rabbit. When the last leaf falls."

Just then, the cub burst from a bush nearby and tumbled into them, sending them sprawling to the floor.

Ernest stood proudly over them, tail high, and asked, "This?"

Cecil got to his feet, looking at what the cub had dropped in front of them. "No, little fox, this is actually a pinecone. But it was a good try."

Ernest wagged his tail, "I try again!" He gave Cecil a quick sniff, then dropped his nose to the muddy floor, disappearing into the woodland.

"Where are you, acorn?" the squirrel said distractedly to no one in particular, as he led the rabbits away from the water. They soon emerged from beneath the treeline and Bunny Hill sprawled out before them. Cecil continued sure pawed across the grass, until he came to an abrupt halt, this time standing right in front of an old, mossy, fallen tree. Wrapper and Bea knew the tree well and had played on it more times than they could remember.

"Oh," said the squirrel in a sad voice, "it fell."

Wrapper was puzzled. The tree had been down as long as he could remember, and much, much before that, he was sure of it. The old squirrel must be even older than he had thought.

"You knew this tree?" Bea asked curiously.

"This is where I used to live, when I was just a tiny little squirrel. They were happy times. I do miss my mother and father, terribly so."

"Where did they go?" asked Wrapper, confused.

"Their leaves fell," he explained, looking at the two rabbits, "a very long time ago."

Suddenly, the cub reappeared, wagging his fluffy orange tail.

"What have you got this time?" asked Bea, and he dropped a stick at their feet.

"Not quite," said Wrapper, "but keep trying!" Ernest quickly snapped up the stick, gave Cecil another sniff and wandered off again, nose low, tail high.

As he continued to mutter about his missing acorn, Wrapper and Bea followed Cecil attentively down the green slope of Bunny Hill, the sun slowly creeping toward the horizon. The squirrel skipped lightly over the slippery surface. *If only Grandrabbit could move so freely*, thought Wrapper in amazement. He pictured the old rabbit hobbling along, his trusty walking stick grasped in his paw.

Cecil stopped at the foot of the hill, next to the gently trickling stream.

"So, is this where you dropped your acorn?" asked Wrapper hopefully.

Cecil looked around, thoughtfully. "No," he said eventually, "No this is somewhere else." A big smile broke over his fluffy little face and his tufty ears wiggled. "This is where I used to play with my little lad!" He gave a happy little hop and ran down to the water. He dipped his toe in, withdrawing it quickly. "It was much warmer then," he smiled fondly, "We used to throw pebbles and go paddling. They really do grow so fast!" He stared happily at the stream, drifting away along happy memories.

Out of nowhere, Ernest landed in the water with a splash, soaking Bea's fur. She shook herself irritably and glared at the cub. The fox however, failed to notice, too excited to show Cecil his latest find. He dropped something onto the damp, earthy bank, that landed with a soft thud.

"Well, it is about the right size, but unfortunately, little cub, this is in fact a little stone."

Ernest began to chase his tail in frustration. Once he'd caught it, he took a big breath, and released himself. "Okay, one more!" he said, and gave the squirrel an almighty sniff and ran off. Cecil picked up the pebble and threw it into the stream, where it landed with a pleasing splash.

They were making their way back up Bunny hill, Ernest's tail occasionally appearing in the air nearby. They passed several trees dotted about the hillside with many rabbits hopping around underneath, talking, playing and generally going about their bunny business. Unfortunately, and most importantly, Wrapper saw no sign of any squirrels, red or otherwise. He looked up at the sky which now had a deep, orange glow. They were running out of time!

Bea gave Wrapper a look. "Sir, we need to get you home," she said gently but firmly to the squirrel, "the sun will soon be asleep." But Cecil did not look concerned.

He turned to her with a smile, and said assuredly,

"Don't worry. I think we might be close." The squirrel scampered off, bushy red tail in the air.

The squirrel eventually stopped in front of the beehives, back toward the top of the hill. "Huh, that's strange," said Cecil abruptly.

"What's that?" asked Bea.

"Well, I'm sure I was here recently, with my granddaughter, and I think I had the acorn." He turned to them both with a proud smile, "She's a terribly clever stick you know, my granddaughter I mean."

"So, what's so strange then?" asked Wrapper, reminding himself to be extra patient.

"Well," he said, with a look of concern, "where did the bees go?"

All too aware of the sun rapidly disappearing behind the hill, Wrapper replied, "The bees have been gone for a long time now. Cecil, we really need to get moving or it will be dark!"

Cecil looked at Wrapper through wise old eyes. "But my dear boy, why rush?" Once more, the squirrel skipped away, almost lost amongst the glow of the setting sun.

Cecil finally came to a stop and the two rabbits found themselves staring up at the Old Oak. It was almost dark now, and much to their surprise they found

Ernest already sitting happily beneath, beating his tail against its mighty trunk.

"Ah yes, of course." A look of understanding spread over the squirrel's old fuzzy face. "Good boy," he said to the fox, giving him a scratch behind the ears.

They rabbits looked at the scene before them.

"This is your acorn?" asked Wrapper, doubtfully.

"Yes. From tiny seeds grow mighty trees. Come, sit with me," Cecil said, settling himself down below the Old Oak. Wrapper and Bea sat either side of him curiously, Ernest plodding over to join them. "I have lived long and happily," said the old squirrel in a contented voice, "and have learnt that life is like a stream, carrying you where it will. It is simply a journey to be enjoyed. Now, here I am at the end of mine. Thank you all for helping me find my way."

"If this is where your journey took you…. where are you going next?" asked Wrapper.

"Why, home of course."

"But…" Bea began, confused.

"Home is not where, young rabbits," Cecil interrupted, a look of meaning in his eyes, "it is who."

Wrapper thought for a moment, as he watched the moon rising, glinting through a gap in the clouds. He looked up at the branches above his head, and at that very moment, the Old Oak gave up its final leaf. The rabbits watched it delicately flutter toward them, eventually coming to rest right between the two friends.

They jumped up in fright. The leaf had landed exactly where Cecil had been sitting, only seconds before… but there was no sign of him.

"Where did he go?" exclaimed Bea, shocked eyes wide.

"I don't know, I didn't see!" replied Wrapper, equally as alarmed. The rabbits were full of worry, and hopped desperately around the great trunk of the oak. Ernest however, remained still and gave a little whine. Wrapper and Bea came to a sudden halt in front of the fox, who was smiling at them from the grass.

"Did you see where he went?" asked Bea, urgently.

Ernest wagged his tail reassuringly. "Squirrel okay now," the cub told them, in a calm, assured tone.

"Where did he go?" asked Wrapper, curiously.

"Home," the fox replied simply.

"Home?" asked Wrapper, uncertainly.

Ernest simply continued to smile, sweeping his tail over the cool, damp earth.

The wise old tree gave a gentle creak as it swayed delicately in the light breeze blowing across the hillside. Wrapper and Bea looked up to see a thousand stars twinkling overhead through dancing branches. They gazed in wonder, bathed in silvery light, magic pouring over them.

Wrapper and friends will return,
with the
Wonders of Winter

Acknowledgments

As with everything, there was more than just one person who contributed to the creation and publication of this book, and this first instalment of *Wrapper the Rabbit* was certainly a team effort.

To start with, I'd like to send some thank you's back in time. Firstly, to my Nanny, Joan Holdstock, who helped me create my first ever '*book*' and the origins of *Wrapper the Rabbit*, many years ago! Secondly, I would like to give a shout out to my old pet rabbits, Gregory and Clementine, who undoubtedly helped inspire these stories.

Back in the present; a very big thank you to my team of proofreaders and editors, who had to wade through my original spelling and grammar mistakes! This includes my Mum and Dad (Graham and Claire Huggins), Katie Checkley, Sue King and her granddaughters Lilith and Eira, Robert Hitch, Lyn Smith-Dennis and Steve Rigby. Thank you all for your help, honest reviews and contributions!

Most importantly I would like to thank my wonderful girlfriend, Beth Jones, who I love very much. Not only have you helped and supported me all the way, as well as having the very first read of every story and influencing each one, but you have also produced some truly beautiful illustrations, which really bring the world to life.

Finally, I would like to thank you; the reader. Without you, Wrapper and his friends would not truly have been brought to life. I hope you have enjoyed your first visit into this world!

About the Author

Who am I? What a question, and one that we all must surely ponder from time to time. On a philosophical level, who are any of us, in the vast beauty of the ever-changing universe. Nothing but star dust and magic! However, with two feet on planet Earth, I am very much me.

Born in Maidstone Hospital, Spring 1994, I'm happy to report that the childhood that followed, was nothing short of magical. Growing up on stories from the likes of J.R.R. Tolkien and J.K. Rowling, the power of words fuelled my young mind. These happy years were spent gleefully running around, heroically slashing at goblins of the imagination. It was during this time, at the age of just 5 years-old, when I wrote my first story.

For close to a decade, I have been fortunate enough to work for Buttercups Sanctuary for Goats, where I have had the privilege of being involved with rescues of all kinds. During my time at the sanctuary, I have also had the pleasure of reporting stories for the quarterly newsletter, which has an audience of several thousand, and reaches all corners of the world.

Now, fuelled by an unquenchable thirst for the mysteries of life, combined with a heart full of dreams, the time is finally right for me to set off on my next adventure; becoming an author.

About the Illustrator

Smart, big-hearted and beautiful, to sum her up. Growing up, Beth enjoyed her fair share of fairy-tales, along with a mild-addiction to the Harry Potter series, and has always been proud of her Scottish roots.

Beth spent four years studying at the University of East Anglia and Imperial College London, completing her masters in Reproductive and Developmental Biology in 2015. She has since worked as a Research Practitioner for the NHS in the south east.

Following a trip to her beloved Switzerland in 2018, where she had a chance encounter with a particularly mischievous goat, Beth decided to join the team at Buttercups Sanctuary for Goats, and has continued to volunteer with the charity since. She also donates some of her time to volunteering with English Heritage, keeping a close eye on stonework older than most of the trees surrounding it.

Beth has been involved with the Wrapper the Rabbit series from the beginning, and is largely the reason the stories are set where they are. Not only has she provided some beautiful illustrations, but she has also had the first read of all the stories, making countless contributions along the way.

About Scotney Castle

The real-world, inspirational setting for the Wrapper stories, is National Trust property Scotney Castle, near Tunbridge Wells, located close to the border between Kent and East Sussex, within the valley of the Bewl river. The property and surrounding estate came into the Trust's care in 1970, although the earliest record of occupancy dates back to 1137.

As well as the mansion, along with the Old Castle island which is set amongst beautiful gardens, Scotney Castle also includes 780 acres of ancient parkland and woodland full of beautiful veteran trees, which are ready to be explored. You may well encounter cattle and sheep grazing the land, as they have since the Victorian times.

The site is well worth a visit, and also has a tea-room, gift shop, second hand book shop, and yes, of course, a beautiful swing beneath an oak tree overlooking the valley.

Lightning Source UK Ltd.
Milton Keynes UK
UKHW011829131121
393907UK00001B/35

9 781800 310209